CLUCK ONE

By Louise Mathews · Pictures by Jeni Bassett

DODD, MEAD & COMPANY · NEW YORK

For Barbara and Larry, two very good eggs — L.M.

To my Grandparents — J.B.

1 2 3 4 5 6 7 8 9 10

Library of Congress Cataloging in Publication Data
Mathews, Louise.
Cluck one.
Summary: As a weasel sneaks an assortment of animal
eggs into Mrs. Cluck's nest, the unaware hen eagerly
awaits their hatching.
[1. Domestic animals — Fiction. 2. Counting]
I. Bassett, Jeni, ill. II. Title.
PZ7.M4253Cl   [E]   81-12532
ISBN 0-396-08029-4   AACR2

"I laid our first egg!" cried Mrs. Cluck,
showing it to the rooster.

"Cluck One, our first little rooster!" he crowed. "I'm going to be a father!"

"So you're counting your chickens before they hatch," honked the goose.

1st

"What's wrong with that?" the hen asked.
"They might be baa-aaaaad," said the sheep.

"Poppycock!" cried Mr. Cluck. "All our
eggs will hatch beautiful chicks and
they will all crow as loudly as I do!"

"Not little roosters!" sighed the weasel,
who liked to snooze in the daytime
so he could make mischief at night.
"The last thing I need is more alarm Clucks
crowing like their father."

That evening when the Clucks were asleep
a cuckoo came to the hen coop.
"Why should I hatch my egg," she said,
"when this hen can do it for me?"
She rolled her spotted blue egg into
the coop, then quietly flew away.

The weasel, out on his nightly prowl,
chuckled as he watched.
"Won't it be fun if the rooster is fooled!
I wonder if he will think a chicken
can hatch from a cuckoo's egg?"

"Look, Mrs. Cluck!" crowed the rooster at dawn.
"You laid an egg in your sleep!"

"I did?" asked the hen in surprise.

"What a marvel you are!" said Mr. Cluck.

"Most hens lay their eggs in the daytime.

But here is Cluck Two, our second small rooster!"

He crowed as he strutted into the barn.

2nd

"That silly rooster!" the weasel laughed.
"He's so easy to fool! I'll play a joke on him, too.
When the eggs *I* give him hatch, won't he be surprised!"
So that day the weasel went to the marsh
and found a green egg among the reeds.
That night he slipped it into the coop.

"Cluck Three, our third little rooster!"
Mr. Cluck crowed early in the morning.

"Have you noticed the third egg is green?"
asked the goat.

3rd

"Oh, dear, it is," peeped Mrs. Cluck.

"And the second egg is blue," mooed the cow.

"We planned it that way," cried the rooster,
 waving his colorful tail like a flag.
"My wife laid those eggs to match my feathers!"

"That's just duckie," chuckled the weasel.

"I think I'll play another prank on Mr. Cock-a-doodler."

The weasel trotted to a garden and

found a shiny egg by a hedge.

That night he put it into the chicken coop.

"Cluck Four, our fourth little rooster!"
Mr. Cluck crowed at dawn.
He held up the shiny egg for all to see.
"It's going to be as handsome as I am!"

4th

"That rooster is as vain as a peacock,"
the weasel laughed to himself.
Then he scurried to the zoo.
When a long-legged bird wasn't looking,
he took a large egg from its cage. That
night he shoved it quietly into the coop.

"Look at Cluck Five, our fifth little rooster,"
Mr. Cluck crowed at sunup. "It's going
to be a giant!"

"I don't see how *you* laid that egg,"
the goose said to the hen.

"It's a puzzle," said Mrs. Cluck.

5th

Mr. Cluck spread out both his wings. "Don't you know, you silly goose, that big eggs mean big roosters?"

"Or big surprises," said the weasel.
"The last egg I'm going to put in their
coop will be the best joke of all."
Then he scampered to the ocean and dug in
the sand until he found a round egg.
That night he rolled it into the coop.

"Cluck Six, our sixth little rooster!
That's half a dozen eggs now,"
Mr. Cluck crowed at sunrise.

"But look how round your last egg is.
It looks like a ball," said the pig.

6th

"Let's see if it bounces," honked the goose, reaching for it with her beak.

"Don't! You'll break it!" cried Mrs. Cluck.

The rooster pushed the goose aside.

"All our eggs will hatch chicks soon.

They don't need your help to crack open," he said.

Then he put fresh straw in the coop.

Every day Mrs. Cluck sat on her nestful of eggs. But she could not cover the largest egg. Mr. Cluck had to warm that one himself.

Then one day the two of them heard
tap-tap-tapping sounds under their wings.
"Our six eggs are hatching!" cried the Clucks.
Everyone in the barnyard crowded around to watch.

1st   2nd   3rd   4th   5th   6th

Cluck One, a yellow chick, popped
from the first egg.
"Cock-a-doodle-doo!" crowed the rooster,
so loudly that everyone jumped.

1st

But then he was quiet and
did not even open his beak,
for Cluck Two, the second egg, hatched a cuckoo,
and Cluck Three, the third egg, was a duck.
"Whoever heard of a chicken quacking?"
said the goat to the cow.

2nd   3rd

Mr. Cluck turned as red as his comb when Cluck Four, the fourth egg, hatched a peacock, and Cluck Five, the fifth egg, was a long-legged ostrich.

"That certainly is a big bird," said the goose.

"It won't even fit in your coop."

4th   5th

"We'll build on more rooms," said the rooster.
"Yes, a new wing," said the hen.

Cluck Six, a turtle, crept from the sixth egg.
"I didn't know chickens were green," said the pig.

"That shell it has on its back
looks baa-aaaaad," said the sheep.

"You counted your chickens before they hatched
and look at them now, **Mr. Cluck**,"
laughed the weasel, leaning over the fence.
"Instead of a family of roosters, you will have . . .

. . . a cuckoo that sings, and a hissing peacock, an ostrich that snorts, and a quacking duck. Maybe your turtle will snap its jaws. But don't count on your one chick crowing. It will probably just peep like a hen."

"Then all our children should sound lovely together," said Mrs. Cluck.

"Yes, they'll make a tremendous racket!" crowed Mr. Cluck, brightening up.

And so they did, from sunup to sundown,
disturbing the weasel's naps much more
than the rooster did at dawn.

"It seems," sighed the weasel, quite annoyed,
"that the last joke is on me."